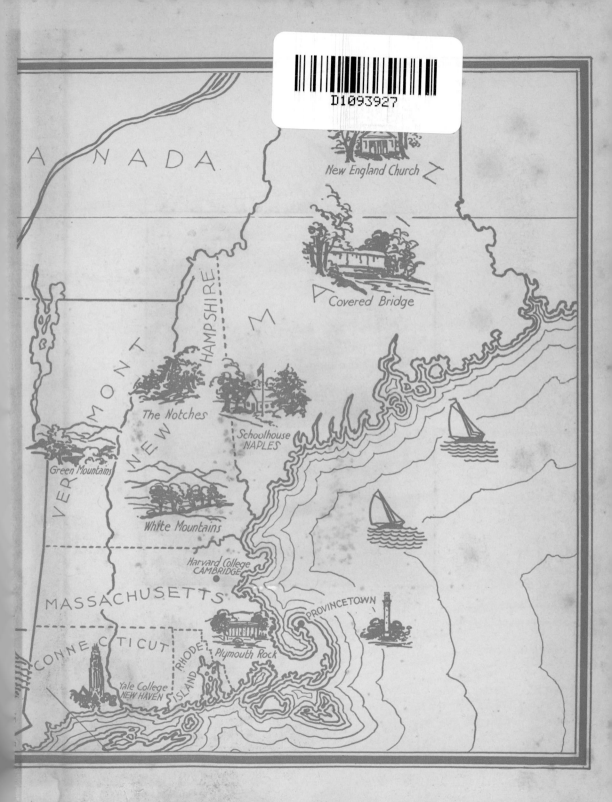

CANADA

New England Church

Covered Bridge

VERMONT

NEW HAMPSHIRE

MAINE

The Notches

Schoolhouse
NAPLES

Green Mountains

White Mountains

Harvard College
CAMBRIDGE

MASSACHUSETTS

PROVINCETOWN

CONNECTICUT

RHODE
ISLAND

Plymouth Rock

Yale College
NEW HAVEN

D1093927

# LITTLE JOHN
## OF
# NEW ENGLAND

SCENE AT PROFILE LAKE, NEW HAMPSHIRE

# LITTLE JOHN OF NEW ENGLAND

BY

MADELINE BRANDEIS

GROSSET & DUNLAP

PUBLISHERS          NEW YORK

COPYRIGHT, 1936, BY
GROSSET & DUNLAP, INC.

*All Rights Reserved*

*Printed in the United States of America*

Dedicated, with love, to Uncle
Lex, who used to be a "good
little devil," too! (and still is!)

# CONTENTS

PAGE

Chapter I
John Makes a Strange Friend . . . . . . . 13

Chapter II
John Tells a Story . . . . . . . . 22

Chapter III
John's Mother Writes a Letter . . . . . . 36

Chapter IV
John Goes to Naples . . . . . . . . 48

Chapter V
John's Mother Writes a Letter . . . . . . 54

Chapter VI
John Has a Bad Afternoon . . . . . . 66

Chapter VII
John's Mother Writes a Letter . . . . . . 75

Chapter VIII
John Goes to School . . . . . . . . 81

Chapter IX
John's Mother Writes a Letter . . . . . . 93

Chapter X
John Has a Surprise . . . . . . . . 101

# CONTENTS

PAGE

Chapter XI

John Goes to Portland . . . . . . . . 109

Chapter XII

John's Mother Writes a Letter . . . . . . 118

Chapter XIII

John Plays with Matches . . . . . . . 129

Chapter XIV

John's Mother Writes a Letter . . . . . . 140

Chapter XV

John Writes a Letter . . . . . . . . 153

## THOSE WHO POSED FOR THE
## ILLUSTRATIONS IN
## "LITTLE JOHN OF NEW ENGLAND"

JOHN .....................BILLY HALL

THE TEACHER ..............DORIS STONE

ROGER BEACON ..............BILLY HUFFER

AUNT PRUE ................ELSIE BISHOP

UNCLE NED ................FRANK PHARR

"C. F." .....:............FREDERICK HUSTON

PAL ......................"TEDDY"

To the two "Billys," to "Doris," "Elsie," "Frank,"
"Frederick," and, last but certainly not least, my
friend, "Teddy," deepest thanks!

MADELINE BRANDEIS

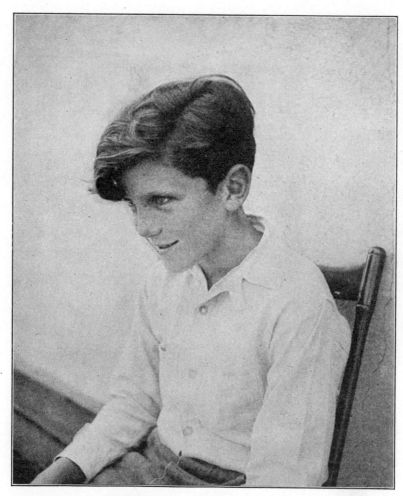

LITTLE JOHN OF NEW ENGLAND

# LITTLE JOHN OF NEW ENGLAND

## CHAPTER I

## JOHN MAKES A STRANGE FRIEND

John sat down on the side of the road and cried. Pal anxiously kissed him with a wet and loving tongue. John put his arm about the small brown and white body of the little bull dog, and Pal cuddled close.

Nothing but busy squirrel rustlings in the nearby trees broke the country stillness of a New England afternoon. The brown road stretched lazily ahead,—the road down which John had just watched his parents' car disappear.

They had left John behind! Left him for the first time in nine years. Of course John did not care very much what had happened before those nine years, because he had not yet been born.  But now he did care.  Most terribly!

He did not want to stay on his uncle's farm.  He was lonesome already.  If it were not that he had Pal with him. . . .  What was that?

John lifted his head and winked the tears out of his eyes.  A car was jogging toward him and it resembled a square, red coffee can!  It was very funny.  But even funnier was the fact that it drew up in front of John, stopped with a sort of whooping cough, and out jumped a little old man.

"Good afternoon," squeaked the stranger, in a factory-whistle voice.

He had a slender, red face, very much like the tender body of a young, unfeathered bird.  He had blue, bright eyes and a sharply pointed white beard.  He stood gazing down at John.

"Do you mind telling me why you were

crying?" he asked, and he seemed to care.

John brushed his sleeve across his brimming eyes and answered, "Because my parents just went away."

"Where did they go?" asked the little man.

"On a motor trip," said John. "Father had to go on business, but they'll have fun, too. I—I wanted to go—along—but—they left me——"

A new crop of tears threatened dangerously, when all of a sudden the stranger gave a leap and landed in a sitting position beside John. Pal growled and showed the whites of his round eyes. But the little man did not seem a bit afraid and patted the dog's head, whereupon Pal stopped growling. The stranger then smiled at John.

"You see," he said, "Your dog understands me. Now, shall we be friends, too?"

He put out a claw-like hand and John clasped it. "That's right!" he squeaked. "Now you may call me 'C. F.'"

"What does it mean?" asked John.

"That is my secret," replied C. F.  "But one day I'll tell you.  Now, have you any secrets?"

John hesitated.  "Well—" he began.

"You need not be afraid of me," said the stranger.  "I am really a splendid old chap! I can see that something is troubling you, so if you'll tell me, perhaps I can help you."

"Will you promise never to speak of it to anyone?" asked John.

C. F. put his bony finger to his lips and mumbled "Mmmm."

"Well," said John.  "There's a treasure at the end of my parents' trip!"

"A treasure?" piped the old man, shrilly.

"Yes, a real treasure," answered John. "It must be hundreds of years old, too.  It was hidden away by Father's ancestors."

C. F. moved up closer to John.  His little pointed, white beard twitched.  His bright eyes sparkled.  If John had only known

C. F. MUMBLED, "MMMM."

why!  But John did not know.  Neither did he realize that by mentioning the treasure he had made his first mistake—a mistake which was to cause him many anxious days.

The little old man cleared his throat. "Why didn't your parents take you along on the trip?" he inquired.

"Because of school," said John, sadly.

C. F. nodded like a wise old hen.  "And where are they going?" he asked.

"Through the New England states," replied John.

"Do you know their names?"

This question so startled John that he jumped.  Did he know his own parents' names?  What an odd little man!

"Why, of course I do, sir!" answered John. "Mr. and Mrs. Jonathon Mason."

"What!"  Now it was the stranger's turn to jump.  He stared hard at John and then began a cackling sort of laugh.  "No, not your parents' names," he said.  "The names of the New England states!"

"Oh!"  John laughed, too.  "Yes, I know them," he replied.  "They're New Hampshire——"

"The Granite State!" interrupted C. F. "State of great mountains and great men, too!"

"Vermont——" continued John.

But C. F. broke in again.  "Green Mountain State!" he exclaimed.  "The name is taken from two French words, 'Vert,' meaning 'green,' and 'mont' meaning 'mountain.' "

"Yes, sir," gulped John, and tried to go on. "Connecticut——"

"The Nutmeg State," cut in C. F. "From an Indian word meaning 'long river.' "

"Rhode Island——"

"Called 'Little Rhody.' Founded by Roger Williams, who was sent out of Massachusetts because he believed that people should pray as they wanted to."

"Maine——"

"This great 'Pine Tree State' of woods and lakes."

"And Massachusetts!" finished John.

"The 'Bay State,' " said C. F. "Name taken from Indian tribe. State of our beginning." Then he turned to John and asked suddenly, "And what is your State?"

"Massachusetts," said John. "I live in Boston."

NAPLES, MAINE

He half expected his new friend to add, "which is New England's largest city. It is called 'The Hub' because the world was supposed to turn around Boston as a wheel turns around a hub!"

But there was silence from C. F. for a change, so John continued, "Mother and

Father brought me up here and left me at
Uncle Ned Hollis' farm.   I have to stay with
Uncle Ned and Aunt Prue until Mother and
Father come back.   I have to go to the coun-
try school and it's so small that I'm sure I'll
never learn a thing!"

"Why won't you learn in a small school as
well as in a large one?" asked C. F.   "Many
a great man went to school up here in the
Maine woods.   I did!"

John wanted to laugh.   The little fellow
did not look like a "great man."   His clothes
were shabby.   His shoes were old.

"But continue," he said.   "I'm ever so interested in your story.   Especially in the
TREASURE!"

He whispered the last word, mysteriously.

## CHAPTER II

## JOHN TELLS A STORY

"Not long ago," began John, "an uncle of Father's died and left us a very, very old house in Boston. It had belonged to our family for generations. It was dark and terribly gloomy——"

"Wait!"

The little old man jumped up with an abrupt bound. "Before you go on with your story," he piped, "we shall make ourselves more comfortable. Come with me!"

They got into C. F.'s funny red coffee-can car, and off they drove together. Pal perched on John's knees and sniffed the soft autumn air.

They jogged through the village of

Naples, a little town with a row of very clean-faced, white houses. Almost every house wore green shutters, a peaked roof and a surprised expression. A sleepy lake with a tiny island in its arms yawned at the town.

The air was so fresh that it made even lakes yawn. It made people very hungry and John, who was always hungry anyway, felt a longing for food. As if in answer to his thoughts, C. F. drew up his car and stopped.

"Here we are!" he squeaked. "This is my abode. Abode really means a home. But this is only a red, ramshackle, rambling ruin, —and if you can think of another word beginning with 'R' to describe it, I'll give you a doughnut!"

John laughed. "I see some relics scattered around," he said.

"Good!" cried C. F. "Ever so good! Those are some of my antiques. And now you may enter and I will give you the doughnut."

Soon the two were seated together on a dusty trunk inside C. F.'s "abode." Both chewed contentedly on their doughnuts, which were the sugared kind that John liked. The place was more a barn than a house. It was piled up high with all sorts of dust-covered objects, such as spinning wheels, rocking chairs, pictures and old-fashioned ornaments.

"As you may have guessed," said C. F., "I am an antique man. I buy, sell, love—in fact, I *am* an antique!"

John knew that antique meant ages old and he wondered whether C. F. could really be that ancient.

"But enough of me!" said the little old man. "On with your story. You were saying that a relative left you an ancestral home. That means your people have always lived in Boston. Doesn't this make you feel proud?"

STREET IN BOSTON, MASS.

"Well, yes," answered John. "But I was going to tell you about the old, gloomy house where we——"

"Boston with her narrow streets," recited C. F., "blackened old buildings, Navy Yard, oldest in the country, and——"

"The house was very gloomy!" shouted John, a determined look in his eye.

Why would this annoying old man keep interrupting him! He had asked for the story of the treasure and——

"Did you know that the Boston subway was the first in America?" continued C. F., talking as much to the wall as to John. "If you wish to go down to that subway, you must walk upstairs. But if you wish to go up to the elevated railway, you must walk downstairs. Isn't that odd?"

John started to open his mouth, but C. F. did not wait for the words to come out. He continued, "What do you think of Boston's alphabet streets? Of course you noticed that Arlington Street, Berkeley Street, Clarendon Street, Dartmouth Street, Exeter Street, Fairfield Street, Gloucester Street, Hereford Street make the A. B. C.'s. And can you tell me what happened on the balcony of the Old State House many years ago?"

John was growing more and more annoyed. What was C. F. trying to do, any-

THE OLD STATE HOUSE, BOSTON, MASS.

way? Give him a school test? He wanted to answer, "No, I can't tell you!" and proceed with his story. But it chanced that John knew the correct reply to C. F.'s question, so how could he help wanting to show his knowledge?

"The Declaration of Independence was read there!" he said.

"Correct," smiled C. F. "But I am sure

you do not know where the lantern was hung for Paul Revere on the night of his famous ride?"

"Yes, I do!" said John, angrily. (What did C. F. think he was, anyway? A first-grade baby?) "It was the Old North Church!"

"Well, I declare!" exclaimed C. F. "You do know a bit! And which building is Boston's only skyscraper?"

"The Customs House," said John, in a disgusted tone. Why wouldn't the silly little man allow him to get on with his story when he had seemed so eager to hear it?

As if in answer to John's thoughts, C. F. suddenly asked, "Well, why don't you tell me about your house?"

Why indeed, thought John! Because of your interruptions! But John remembered his friend's age and checked his anger.

"Even though the house was gloomy," he

said, "I liked it because my ancestors lived there when they were children. I used to wonder what sort they had been and what they had done in those days when the house was new. So you can understand how I felt when we discovered the secret door!"

"No, I cannot understand at all!" said C. F. "And I do not even know what door you are talking about!"

"It was a secret door to a closet which had been sealed up for years and years," explained John. "Mother found it by accident one day when she was exploring. Because, you know, there were so many corners and cubbyholes and strange places."

"In that closet we found an old-fashioned bonnet and other things that Mother and Father said were 'interesting.' But the map was my favorite. It was colored and full of pictures and directions and underneath were the words:

"We are hiding a treasure for our descendants of the Twentieth Century. When that Century comes around, he who finds this map will know that the treasure is for him! Seek it and accept it with the love of your ancestors MARY, WILLIAM, AND NED MASON."

"Mother said that it was only a silly joke played by some children, and Father said 'Pooh!' But I studied that map and studied it!"

John's companion seemed to have gone into a dream. "I can just see those three children of olden times," he said. "The girl with her long, full skirts, the boys in their short, tight jackets and long trousers.

"And what an interesting age they lived in! Day of the first railroad in America! Day of the famous clipper ships,—those long, low sailing vessels. How proud our ancestors were of them! Boston a young, growing city. Not at all as it is today.

"Why, on the site of the Hotel Touraine, John Adams, our second President, once lived. Today, as you know, modern traffic is thick in that part of the city. But years ago, Mr. Adams moved away from there because he said that the noisy traffic disturbed him. Just imagine, six wagons passed every hour!"

C. F. laughed, but John scowled. More interruptions! And besides, he knew just as much about Boston as C. F. did! Maybe more! He had seen Paul Revere's house, and the Bunker Hill Monument on Breed's Hill, where the Battle of Bunker Hill took place.

He had been to the Old Granary Burying Ground where so many famous people lie buried. It always amused him that Paul Revere appeared to have two graves there. In one spot it announced that "Paul Revere Lies Here," while in another, the marker read, "Here Lies Paul Revere." One is, no doubt, the grave of his son.

"What are you thinking of?" asked C. F. "And why don't you go on with your story?"

John was on the point of answering, "Because you keep interrupting me!" But again he remembered respect for older people.

"I studied that map," he continued, "until I was sure I could picture in my mind just where the treasure had been hidden."

"Where?" asked C. F. sharply.

And then John made his second mistake.

"Out on the tip of Cape Cod," he answered. "In Provincetown."

C. F. looked at John curiously. "Will your parents go there?" he asked.

John gazed down at the floor. "I'm not at all sure," he replied. "Mother promised to try and persuade Father to go. But, you see, Father always laughs at my map and calls it 'John's mystery-story!' Whenever Mother and I talk about the treasure he tiptoes

C. F. STARED STRAIGHT AHEAD OF HIM.

around, saying 'Hush!' Mother tries not to laugh, but I know it's only because she doesn't want to hurt my feelings."

"Are you sure there is a treasure out there?" asked C. F.

"Yes, I am," answered John. "And I know it's for me!"

At this, John noticed C. F. suddenly change. His face took on a sober, stern look. He was not at all the same, eager, cheerful person he had been.   He put one finger to his lips and stared straight ahead of him.

All at once John grew afraid.   Should he have told C. F. his story?   Who was this old man anyway?   Why, John didn't even know what those strange initials, C. F., stood for! And then, this funny barn full of antiques! What did it all mean?

John slid down off the trunk.   "I'd better be going home, I think," he said.

Not a word from C. F. as John moved toward the door, followed by Pal.

"And—and thank you for the doughnut," he added, politely.

Still silence from C. F.   But just as John reached the door, the little fellow jumped down off the trunk and ran after him.

"Wait!" he squealed.   "Did you say that the map led to Provincetown on Cape Cod?"

"Yes," answered John.

"And where are your parents going first?"

"To the White Mountains in New Hampshire."

"What kind of car are they in?"

"A long, cream-colored roadster."

"And where will they stop tonight?"

"Ports—" But suddenly John stopped without finishing the word. He began to realize what a foolish thing he had been doing. Why should he tell this stranger everything? What reason had C. F. for being so curious about John's parents and the treasure? Yes, especially about the treasure!

"Ports—what? Ports—what?" screeched C. F.

"I won't tell you!" cried John, and ran out of the barn as fast as he could run, Pal barking at his heels.

## CHAPTER III

# JOHN'S MOTHER WRITES A LETTER

My dear Son:

*When we drove away and left you yesterday, your father and I felt very sad. We did so wish that you could have gone along with us, and we wish it more and more the further we push into this glorious New England country!*

*Strange to have lived so many years in Boston and never to have known what a fairyland lay around us all the time. Of course when I was a child I used to visit the Maine woods where you are now staying. I hope, dear, that you will love the fresh, open country, the lakes and trees, as much as I did.*

*But I know that you are longing to hear*

*about your precious map, and so let me as-sure you that it is safe!  Also, Father says he is willing to follow the lead of your "treas-ure" to Cape Cod at the end of our journey, if there is time!*

*And, by the way, I have a rather exciting adventure to tell you about before I close this letter.  It is an adventure which I know you will like because—well, because you are my Johnny and love mysteries as I do!*

*But before I tell you of "the noise at night," and the "strange face of a little old man at the window," I want to describe our journey thus far.  You know, I promised to write you about everything—places, impres-sions, historic spots.*

*In the town of Fryeburg we were shown an old tree which they call the "doughnut tree."  That is because it is twisted into the shape of a doughnut.  You would have been interested, but possibly disappointed because*

THE DOUGHNUT TREE

*you could not have eaten it!*

*Our next stop would have interested you even more. We visited the famous Chinook Kennels, where Eskimo dogs are raised for Antarctic expeditions. We were shown many types of dogs, some with white eyes which the guide explained is a protection against long, snowy days.*

*Some of those dogs have been heroes and have rescued men.   One had been born on an expedition.*

ESKIMO PUPPIES AT THE CHINOOK KENNELS

*Then we drove through the White Mountains of New Hampshire.   What unexpected things do happen along a New England motor road!   Suddenly, among the green, green trees, we saw leaves that might have been fragile glass flames.   And there in a field would magically appear a giant boulder, carelessly covered with a crimson, flower-made coverlet.   Funny, quaint wells and tiny, prim farm gardens!*

FLUME CASCADE IN THE WHITE MOUNTAINS

*Crawford and Franconia Notches are great gashes between the White Mountains. At certain spots, roaring cascades, like silver tornadoes, crash down the mountain sides.*

*Then came Profile Lake, which raises its grey beauty to one of the most amazing sights of all,—The Old Man of the Mountain. It is a carved, stone face, looking as though a spirit-sculptor had chiseled it with giant tools.*

*The White Mountains seem to be dressed in woolly, pine-tree coats up to their necks, their pale faces of granite showing above.*

*We drove through miles of tourist land. Big, comfortable hotels, like pleasant housemaids, held out their porchy arms to tired travellers. But we did not stop at any. We wanted to reach Portsmouth.*

*However, we first passed through Exeter and visited the boys' preparatory school, Phillips Exeter Academy. Its red brick buildings are models of neatness, with their sugar-frosted trimmings. We were told that the students sit around large tables and talk things over instead of having small desks of their own.*

*At last we reached Portsmouth. We saw the house of John Paul Jones, who built that famous old ship, The Ranger. He sailed to Europe in the days of The Revolution and received from a war vessel the first salute ever given the new American flag.*

*We were also shown the home of Thomas Bailey Aldrich who wrote "The Story of a Bad Boy." (And that reminds me of you, John! I hope you are not causing Aunt Prue and Uncle Ned any trouble. Remember, they are not used to boys!)*

*Portsmouth is New Hampshire's only seaport. It used to be the most important navy yard for the building of submarines.*

*We were very tired and went to bed early in a farmhouse near the town. In this coun-*

THE HOME OF THOMAS BAILEY ALDRICH

*try almost every other house seems to have a sign out, inviting tourists to spend the night!*

*And now, here we go on my adventure, so hold your hat, Johnny boy!*

*It must have been around midnight when I heard footsteps outside my window. Our room was on the ground floor of the house.*

*I listened for a while and then it seemed*

*to me that I saw something moving outside of that window. I kept very quiet, and pretty soon I felt positive that I saw a face peering into the room! I was about to awaken your father, when the face disappeared.*

*I lay awake a long time thinking about it. It had been a bearded, thin face; that of an old man, I think. But, in the morning, when I told your father about it, he just laughed and said, "Now I see where John gets his mystery-story mind!"*

*Well, perhaps I was mistaken, but it does make a good story, and I knew you would enjoy it.*

*There are three memory collections one might make while travelling through New England. One would be a collection of famous authors, another of famous schools, and another of famous historic spots.*

*As you know, it was in New England that America really had its beginning. The English king was jealous of Spain, which had made so many discoveries in the new world. So he sent John Cabot, an Italian sailor, across the ocean, and Cabot found the shores of New England which he took for Old England.*

*Then came John Smith, who made a map and gave the country its name. But he declared that never would anyone want to live in this rocky land, except perhaps, to make money.*

*We know that he was wrong, because the first people to settle here were the Pilgrims. They came seeking a land where they could pray in their own way.*

*Is it any wonder that New Englanders are proud of their history? The ages of buildings, names of famous men, dates of battles, are seen on many signs as one drives through villages.*

*And these villages are like little play towns. Many are set among groves of glorious trees, and the whole country is a vacation*

PROFILE LAKE, NEW HAMPSHIRE

*land. Everyone knows that, but I often wonder how it must feel to live in the center of "vacation land" all the year around! In winter the snow is deep and everything must look like a Christmas postcard!*

*Each town and city has its common, or center, around which it lives its life. Some of the houses have the most curious designs over their doors. They are fan shaped and look like the pleated underneath part of a mushroom.*

*We sometimes pass scenes of such beauty that they are almost unreal. For instance, we saw a forest full of shimmering colors— greens, yellows, dappled with speckled sunlight. I held my breath and waited for Puck to break through the branches, or Peter Pan to pick the mottled leaves and make himself a suit.*

*I shall have another letter for you soon, and until then, all the love of your devoted father and*

MOTHER

*P.S. If you have some love left over, after you take all you can use for yourself, give it to Aunt Prue and Uncle Ned. And, oh yes, a package of love pats for Pal!*

CHAPTER IV

## JOHN GOES TO NAPLES

John had puzzled a great deal over his mother's letter. It had worried and frightened him. He was certain that his mother had seen a face at the window that night, and he felt no doubt as to whom that face belonged! He had written a long letter, warning his mother of C. F., and of the little man's interest in the map which led to the treasure.

When John awoke in the mornings, the first thing that met his eyes was the fancy wallpaper pattern in his tiny room. On it were pictures of rose baskets with roses spilling out. The ceiling came slanting down on one side of the room. John thought of the

48

fun bugs and flies might have had using it for a slide, if only they had had sense enough!

There was a woolly rag rug on the floor, and in a corner, a big, white wash bowl. The

UNCLE NED'S FARM

only other furniture was John's small, iron bed and a rocking chair.

Through his window John could see some of the many trees that covered his uncle's farm. He could also see the large wooden barn which needed painting.

He stretched and jumped out of bed. Soon school would start, but today he was still free

to wander about with Pal. He washed his
face. He washed it very carefully because
he knew that if he didn't, Aunt Prue would
send him upstairs to do it over again.

Aunt Prue was a very clean-minded lady.
She was tall and thin and looked much like
the stiff, grandfather's clock in the hall.

When John had scrubbed himself to the
color of a ripe tomato he put on his clothes
and went downstairs. Uncle Ned was already seated at the breakfast table. Uncle
Ned was a farmer and arose early. John sat
down and said "Good morning," and Uncle
Ned said "Good morning" in a deep, mournful voice.

But John was not at all mournful. He
smiled. Not at Uncle Ned, however, but at
the food spread out on the table! Codfish
cakes! Apple pie! Sausages! Fresh, sweet
milk! Poor John! Let him enjoy himself
while he can, for it will not last long!

After breakfast John, his belt loosened,

started right off for the town of Naples. Pal went along, of course. Because John and Pal belonged together, more or less like ham and eggs or sausage and buckwheat cakes!

John wanted to find out whether the face which his mother had seen at the window could really have been C. F.'s. He had not ventured near the old man's house since the strange afternoon he had spent there. But now he walked briskly down the tree-lined street of the village with one idea in his mind. Was C. F. at home?

He stopped before the barn-like building, which C. F. had called his "red, ramshackle, rambling ruin." It looked deserted. The spinning wheel which had been out in front was there no longer.

John walked up to the door. Should he rap? Afraid? Coward! What harm could the little man do him? Still, he had not feared C. F. for himself, but for the treasure! The stranger had shown too great an interest in John's story. And now his mother's letter had made him more uneasy than ever.

He rapped. Nobody answered. He rapped again. Still silence from within. But just as John was turning to go away, a window opened in the house next door and a woman thrust her head out.

"Are you looking for the Antique Man?" she asked.

John told her that he was, and the woman said, "He left suddenly a few days ago and don't ask me where he went for I'm sure I don't know!"

"Did he drive away in a red car?" asked John.

"Yes, he did," replied the woman. "And an odd looking creature it is! But there, he's an odd old fellow himself, as everyone knows!"

John felt cold, as if the morning sun had stopped shining. "You—you're sure nobody would know where he went?" he inquired.

"I'm quite sure!" the woman answered, firmly. "He never tells of his doings, and nobody in the village has ever been able to figure him out!"

As John walked home, the woman's words —"He's an odd old fellow, as everyone knows!"—kept going through his troubled mind. There was no more doubt that C. F. had been interested in the treasure! And perhaps not so honestly interested, either!

He had told John that he loved antiques, and surely the treasure must be very old and very valuable. He had asked John where his parents were going and John had foolishly informed him. Now he was following them in order to—What?

Oh, how John wished that he had not talked so much!

## CHAPTER V

## JOHN'S MOTHER WRITES A LETTER

DEAR JOHN:

*Your letter about the little old man called C. F. gave me quite a shock. And what happened yesterday added greatly to that shock! It also thickens our mystery! But, of course, I dare not tell Father how excited I am, because you know how easily Father says "Pooh!"*

*Yes, Johnny, another strange thing has occurred! No, two strange things! But, wait! I shall take them in their order.*

*We started out in the morning and drove through Gloucester, a little hilly town, weary with age. Do towns ever remind you of people? Well, Gloucester reminded me of a*

THE HARBOR, GLOUCESTER, MASS.

weather-beaten, hump-backed old fisher-
man. Perhaps this was because I knew it to
be a fishing town.

Next we visited Salem, and to those who
love mystery, this is surely the "spookiest"
of places! Firstly, most of the houses are
dull and grey, with shutters that look as if
they would rattle horribly in a wind. They

*seem to be leering at one with a ghostly smile, and their peaked roofs resemble witches' hats.*

*But how silly! All this must surely have been my imagination because of what happened in Salem several hundred years ago. Also, it may have been because of what occurred there yesterday—to me!*

*You know, of course, that Salem is where witchcraft started. In the seventeenth century a group of children were supposed to have been bewitched by two poor old women. This began a frightful state of affairs when many innocent persons were accused of being witches and were executed or thrown into jail.*

*Once, when some milk mysteriously turned sour, it was blamed on a crazy old woman and she was condemned to be hanged.*

*But, finally the Governor's wife was accused of witchcraft, and then the Governor released all the victims! When trouble*

THE WITCH JAIL IN SALEM, MASS.

*strikes our own dear ones, we somehow feel different about things, don't we?*

*And that is why, no doubt, I shiver when I think of the Witch Jail in Salem! Oh, not that I was thrown into one of those gloomy cells where the poor women of olden times had to sit, awaiting their trials. No, those horrible days are over, and anyway, I do not think I look like a witch! Unless, of course, there were plump, rosy-cheeked witches!*

*But enough of this foolishness! We were*

*Courtesy of Karl Maynard.*

NATHANIEL HAWTHORNE'S "HOUSE OF SEVEN GABLES," IN SALEM, MASS.

*shown through the Witch Jail, and when we came out, whom do you think I saw?  That same little old man whose face had peered through the window the other night!*

*Yes, there he was, standing on the opposite side of the street beside a red, cracker-box of a car.  He was looking at me.  But, almost immediately, he hopped into that car and drove away!*

*I was certainly amazed.  And especially after what you had written!  But don't worry about the map, Johnny dear, because I am taking ever such good care of it.  And, anyway, the funny old man may only be a bit queer in the head and entirely harmless.*

*However, I would not tell your father about it, as I know he would say that it was not C. F. who was queer in the head—but I! He might even have me thrown into jail as a witch!  Dear me!*

*But I must get on with this account, for I have more to tell of my adventures with*

*C. F. (By the way, what do you suppose those initials stand for?)*

*From Salem we drove through Lexington and Concord, and of course I need not describe these historic places to you because you have been there yourself.  But while Father called upon business friends, I wandered about.*

*While sitting beside the Old North Bridge in Concord, I thought with pride of the famous battle which was fought there in 1775. I gazed at the statue of the Minute Man who had served his country so bravely and at a minute's notice.*

*I thought of Paul Revere, who was a Minute Man, and of his story about which Mr. Longfellow, the poet, asks you to:*

> *"Listen, my children, and you shall hear
> Of the midnight ride of Paul Revere."*

*Yes, I know you have "listened" and "heard" many times how Paul Revere rode*

OLD NORTH BRIDGE, CONCORD, MASS.

*through the night, waking the countryside and arousing other Minute Men.*

*At Lexington, where the two armies met, the English commanded the Americans to lay down their arms. They refused. The English were the first to fire. Seven Lexington men were killed, and the English marched on.*

*But from every farm sprang angry Rebels.*

*From every bush rained bullets. The story goes that one of the "Red Coats" (as the English soldiers were called) sprang at a Minute Man, fired his gun, and cried, "You are a dead man!" The American, also firing, replied, "So are you!" and both dropped dead!*

*Before we left Concord we paid a visit to the home of Louisa M. Alcott. We stood right in the old parlor which she described in her beautiful book, "Little Women." We walked up the same steps that Amy, Beth, Meg and Jo once used.*

*We were shown into the rooms where these beloved young people had lived. On the wall in Jo's room—(or, rather Louisa's, for the author really was Jo,—) are painted some gay flowers. We were told that Amy did this one day when Jo was ill. They were too poor to buy real flowers, "But, anyway," Amy had said, "real ones would fade, and these will not!"*

LONGFELLOW'S BEDROOM AT "THE WAYSIDE INN,"
SOUTH SUDBURY, MASS.

The next place of interest was "Mary's Little Lamb School House." Once upon a time there was a real Mary and a real little lamb. This old, red schoolhouse is where the story actually took place.

Nearby is The Wayside Inn, made famous by Mr. Longfellow's "Tales of a Wayside Inn." Here we were guided through rooms full of souvenirs. One that would have *pleased you was a large cookie mold with the seal of the United States imprinted on it.*

*How would you like to eat such a patriotic cookie?  I can hear you answering, "I would eat any cookie, whether it were patriotic or not!"  I believe you, my son!*

*As we were being guided around, a most startling thing happened.  At least, it was startling to me.  With the other tourists, we were examining a large, wooden chest which is called a "hutch."  It looked a great deal like the one which your Aunt Prue has in the hallway of her house.  If you don't remember, go and look at it.*

*I was gazing down at the fine old piece of furniture, when I heard a squeaky voice in the crowd say, "What a splendid chest to hide a treasure in, I declare!"*

*The other tourists laughed.  But I did not. The one who had spoken those words was none other than—C. F.!*

*Father is calling me.  We must hurry off
again.  But please do not worry, my dear,
for I have the map tucked safely in my hand-
bag!*

*Your loving, rushing*

MOTHER.

THE WAYSIDE INN

## CHAPTER VI

## JOHN HAS A BAD AFTERNOON

Sitting on the steps of the Naples post office with Pal by his side, John read and re-read his mother's letter. He puzzled and pondered over it.

Then, all of a sudden, up he jumped, as though he had just remembered something of great importance. And so he had! It was time for midday dinner at the farm! John and his appetite started rapidly toward home!

John was met at the door by Aunt Prue, who was crying. It seemed rather funny to John to see a tall, straight, grandfather's-clock-lady crying. But the next thing that happened did not seem funny at all.

Aunt Prue gave a deep sigh, moaned "Oh, my soul and body!" and fled into the house, her apron to her eyes. Then, John heard Uncle Ned's bass voice from inside, calling him. He entered and found Uncle Ned sitting in the parlor with a Bible on his knee. Uncle Ned often read the Bible. He often went to church, too, though he called it "the meeting house."

"Come here to me, John," said Uncle Ned, and John came closer.

What could be the matter? Something dreadful must have happened!

"It is about that dog of yours, John," said Uncle Ned. He glanced at Pal, who was panting like a busy engine, his pink tongue trailing. "Pal has caused Aunt Prue a great deal of trouble since you arrived here."

Now John began to understand. It was true that Pal had been very naughty. He had broken into the chicken yard and killed three chickens. He had chased the cows and

AUNT PRUE

UNCLE NED

frightened the horse and broken a vase.
John waited silently for Uncle Ned's next
words.

"This morning," he continued, "Aunt
Prue found her best quilt torn into shreds.
It was made by her great-grandmother and

she thought much of it.  But she feels sorry for you and could not bear to tell you what we have decided to do.  So I shall have to tell you.  Your dog must go, John!"

"Oh, but Uncle Ned—" began poor John, pitifully.

Uncle Ned went on without even listening to the boy.  "Pal is not a farm dog," he said. "He belongs in a town.  So, today after dinner, I shall drive him into Naples and leave him there with a friend until you return to Boston."

"Oh, but Uncle Ned!" repeated John, and this time his voice was even more pitiful.

"That will be an end to it, John!" said Uncle Ned.

Now, when Uncle Ned said "That will be an end to it!" there usually was.  Uncle Ned had fiery, honest blue eyes, overtopped by grey, bushy eyebrows.  His ancestors had been Puritans, who were very stern and did not allow people to laugh out loud or to dance on Sundays. Those who did were whipped at a whipping post in public. They were also put into the stocks, which were wooden frames with holes for hands and feet.

One felt like addressing Uncle Ned Hollis by the old Puritan name "Goodman Hollis." And, down deep, Uncle Ned was good. Like his Puritan ancestors, he really had a kind and charitable nature.

If he had known about the hurt in John's heart just then, he would never have done what he did. But Uncle Ned did not realize what a very sad thing it was for a little boy who was lonesome already, to lose his dog.

Perhaps Pal had been homesick, too, and that was why he had killed chickens and destroyed things. For Pal had always been a good little dog.

John could not eat his dinner. And that is the same as saying that John was dreadfully upset!

After dinner Uncle Ned went to the barn

to make ready for his trip to town. He was
going to drive his wagon and take some of
Aunt Prue's Rhode Island Red chickens to
sell. He was also going to take Pal, and
John knew that he would not see his pet
again for many weeks.

Now, John was not disobedient—well, not
usually. And he had always respected older
people—well, nearly always. But bad days,
with bad things happening in them, are apt
to make bad boys—at least to make a
difference in a good boy!

John stood in the hall, holding his dog in
his arms. He heard Uncle Ned walking
around outside. He gazed about the small
hallway. There was a crooked staircase in
one corner and a grandfather's clock tick-
ing away in the other. The house smelled
of clean linen and baking.

A large, wooden chest stood against the
side of the wall. Aunt Prue called it her
"hutch table," and it had been handed down

from some ancestor. It was the one John's mother had mentioned in her letter. He now recalled her words:

"I heard a squeaky voice say, 'What a splendid chest to hide a treasure in, I declare!'"

Why, of course! Pal was a treasure, wasn't he? And Pal would fit inside the "hutch!" And there were Uncle Ned's footsteps coming closer and closer. . . .

"Where is the dog, John?"

Uncle Ned's honest eyes looked into John's, and John felt very small. He did not answer.

"Very well, then," said Uncle Ned. "I shall have to look for him."

He strode out of the hall and into the back part of the house, and here was John's chance! He opened the "hutch" and started to lift Pal out of it. He would take him away —far away—he didn't know where, or how, or——

Footsteps!   Back popped Pal, into the
"hutch," and the lid closed.

"Where is that dog, John?" asked Aunt
Prue.  She stood over John like a stiff pine
tree with red eyes.  "If I didn't know you
were an honest boy, I should think you
had——"

An awful howl from within the "hutch"!
Poor John!

Uncle Ned came in, and neither he nor
Aunt Prue said a word to John as they lifted
Pal out.  Then Uncle Ned walked off with
Pal in his arms.

Soon John heard the farm wagon drive
away.  He dared not look out of the window,
because he knew what he would see.  He
would see Pal sitting up beside Uncle Ned
and gazing back at the house, wondering
why John did not come.

And John could not explain!  He felt as if
he had deceived his friend!  He covered his

eyes with his hands and just then he heard a pitiful howl.

John dashed out of the house and as he started blindly through the back door, he ran right into Aunt Prue. He knocked a pitcher of milk out of her hands.

"Land o' mercy!" she screamed.

But John kept right on running. He followed Uncle Ned's wagon until he had reached the side of it.

"Oh, Uncle Ned!" he gasped, "please— please don't take Pal away!"

Uncle Ned looked astonished to see him there and Pal let out a series of frightful, yelpy barks.

"Go home, John," said Uncle Ned. "I told you that there was to be an end to all this! Now mind!"

John stopped in the middle of the road and stood like a poor, forlorn statue until the wagon and Pal's howls were out of sight and sound.

## CHAPTER VII

## JOHN'S MOTHER WRITES A LETTER

DEAR SON:

*I am sorry to have had to leave you so abruptly in my last letter. We were late in getting started and your father had business to attend to in Worcester. This is a tree-decorated city, busy and industrial, with very fine homes and wide streets.*

*Nothing of a mysterious nature happened in Worcester and I did not see your strange friend. But wait! I have a terrible tale to tell you before I am through!*

*We left Worcester and our first stop was made at a place between East Princeton and Westminster. Here, off the road a way, is a big, black rock which is called "Redemp-*

75

*tion Rock." This is the way it got its name:*

*During an Indian attack, the wife of a preacher was carried away by the Redmen. Months later she was rescued here at this rock, and the Indians were paid for her redemption.*

*We passed by the woods of straight, dense trees, like rigid, tall Indians who used to scout among them. I thought of those first white settlers and the peril in which they had lived upon this land, while we rolled easily along, over a safe, smooth road.*

*Did I say "safe?" Well, just at that moment whom do you think I saw? C. F.! There, ahead of us, was his funny red cracker-tin car, going faster than I had any idea it could go. But of course, we passed him, and as we did, the little old man leaned out of the window and stared hard at us.*

*Now, there are not many cream-colored cars like Father's on the road! And I think it is the only one with a bronze monkey sitting up on the radiator cap holding a lighted lantern! So, no wonder it is easy for C. F. to trail us! Oh, I do wish your father's taste were not so different from other people's!*

THE HOBBY HORSE AT THE TOY TOWN TAVERN

*But I said nothing to Father—then. However, Johnny dear, I was obliged, finally, to tell him the whole story, as you will hear! For the worst is yet to come!*

*We drove through more green, tree-covered country. Did you ever notice that the trunks of thin, white birch trees are very like the thin, spindling legs of spider-monkeys?*

*The name of a farm, "Justamere Farm," amused me, and our next stop, Winchendon, delighted me. This is the place where toys are made, and on the golf course of the Toy Town Tavern is the most enormous hobby horse I ever saw!*

*Soon after leaving Winchendon, we crossed the Massachusetts State Line and were in the State of Vermont. In the town of Keane we remarked upon the wide streets and were told this story:*

*It seems that in the olden days the streets were too narrow and the people wanted them widened. So each citizen gave some of his land in the front of his house, but he also took that much land in the back.*

*Camping country! The name, "Thisldu" for a group of cabins, I thought very good, because almost anything will "do" when one is roughing it!*

A VERMONT COVERED BRIDGE

*Have you ever seen a covered bridge? They are long, wooden, barn-like tunnels and we passed quite a few of them. We also passed stands where maple sugar was being sold—real Vermont maple sugar! But I should never dare tell you this had I not sent you a big box, for I know you would pack up at once and come to Vermont to sample it!*

*Trees and water and foliage for miles! Then Brattleboro, a town built on hills. And now again, Massachusetts, passing barns with tobacco hanging up to dry.*

*Deerfield, scene of massacres. One night the French and the Indians attacked the town, killing and capturing men, women and children, burning almost every house.*

*But, today, Deerfield is peaceful. Great, fine trees droop in prayer, and the town itself is sleepy with memories.*

*I wish I could finish describing the rest of our trip up to the present time, and also tell you of my terrifying adventure. But Father is roaring for his dinner! (I think you are like your father in some ways, John!)*

*So, I shall have to close now and write the rest to you after Father has been fed!*

*Until later,*

*Hastily,*
MOTHER.
*And hungrily, Father!*

## CHAPTER VIII

## JOHN GOES TO SCHOOL

John did not want to go to a country school. His Boston school had been large and fine, with a different teacher for every class. The one he was going to had one room and one teacher for all the grades.

John pulled on his cap with a gesture of disgust. He started out of the house. The air had electricity in it. A few fluffy clouds, like dirty cream puffs, hung over the lake as he walked down the quiet country road.

The schoolhouse was set beside the road in the midst of some pine trees. It was a little yellow building and looked more like a tool house than a schoolhouse!

John scowled. Well, fortunately for him,

he would not have to stay here long! His parents would be away only a few weeks and then he could go back to Boston.

John had just written to his mother imploring her to guard the map most carefully. How he should like to be travelling with his parents instead of sitting here in this crowded, country schoolroom!

He was feeling angry and rebellious. He thought of the Rebels in the Revolutionary War! Yes, rebellious! Not, of course, like the Colonists, who had wanted to break away from England, for he only wanted to break away from a school!

John glanced around the room. There were blackboards on all four walls and an old, tin stove in one corner. The teacher's table stood stiffly in front of the row of desks. But the teacher had not yet arrived.

There were little first grade children in the first row. There were older ones in the next row, and at the far end of the room, were

THE NAPLES SCHOOL, NAPLES, MAINE

two girls as tall as Aunt Prue!  Funny school, thought John.

He began to wonder what the teacher would be like, when a boy next to him touched his arm.

"What's your name?" he asked.  He was plump and shiny cheeked.  His clothes fitted him like the skin on an onion.

"John Mason. What's yours?" asked John.

"Roger Beacon. My father's President of the School Board!" He said it proudly and he looked John up and down. "Where do you come from?" he finally asked.

"Boston," answered John. He thought this information would gain Roger Beacon's respect. But instead, it only made him smile.

"Where are your glasses?" he asked John, mockingly.

John did not understand. He did not know that Boston boys are supposed to be very studious and prim. They are often pictured wearing horn-rimmed spectacles.

But John was not at all like this. He did not wear glasses. His straw-colored hair never stayed in place, and his nose was peppered with freckles. Besides, he now wore that "first-day-of-school" expression which, on any boy's face, is never sweet!

"Oh, here comes Teacher!" said Roger, and John heard a sound out in the hallway. Roger leaned closer to John and whispered, "He's a horrid old man with a black beard and he raps our fingers with a ruler if we're not good!"

The pupils straightened up and stopped talking. Roger slid back to the center of his desk. John stiffened. The idea of rapping children's fingers! The horrid old . . .

And then, through the door walked—not a "horrid old man" at all, but a pretty, golden-haired young woman!

"Good morning, children," she smiled.

"Good morning, Miss Wells," replied the class.

John was so astonished that he blurted out loud, "But he—he's a lady!"

It was a long time before the class stopped laughing. In fact, the teacher joined right in and laughed with the children. But not unkindly.

When she heard that John came from Boston, she said, "In honor of John, our lesson today will be about Boston."

Then she took them back to the days when Boston was a small town with a pasture in the center. When little boys wore long hair tied back with ribbons.

The laws of England were very hard upon the Colonists. King George needed money, so he told the Americans that they must pay him something on every pound of tea which arrived from England.

When the King sent some ships filled with tea to Boston Harbor, fifty men dressed up as Indians, with feathers and war paint, and climbed aboard. War-whooping, they threw the tea into the water. This strange "tea-party" was the beginning of the Revolution and is always called "the Boston Tea Party."

When the teacher stopped talking, John decided that he had been much too quiet. Why, he had decided not to like this school!

And here he was being interested! And in something he already knew! Miss Wells talked like a story-book, that was why!

He looked around at Roger Beacon. The stout boy's mouth was open and he was gaping up at the teacher, stupidly. Imagine saying that Miss Wells was a horrid old man with a black beard!

John decided that there was one thing to do about Roger Beacon, and he did it! He picked up a large eraser from his desk and dropped it into Roger's open mouth.

Roger sputtered and made a terrible fuss, and the class started to laugh. But Miss Wells rapped on her desk and looked severely at John, while she continued with her history lesson.

"Some say that the Revolution was really started by a small boy!" She seemed to be saying this directly to John, as though she believed him to have been that boy!

"The English King sent many soldiers to

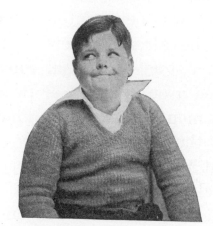

ROGER MADE A TERRIBLE FUSS.

Boston," she went on. "They paraded up and down the little pasture, which is now Boston Common. Their bright red coats shone in the sun.

"One day a barber's boy pointed to an English captain and shouted, 'That mean fellow did not pay my master for curling his hair!'

"The English captain furiously sprang forward and struck the lad with his fist. The angry mob at once surrounded the English captain and began to shout, 'Kill him! Kill him!'

"They threw sticks and stones and very soon there was a wild revolt.

" 'Bloody coats! Lobster Backs!' shouted the Americans. Bells began to ring all over the town and drums to beat. This was the Boston Massacre.

"But today," finished the teacher, "Boston is a dignified and important city. Can anyone tell me some of the things it is noted for?"

"Its battle grounds and monuments," said a girl in the last row.

"Its Boston bulldogs!" piped the voice of a tiny child in the front of the room.

Miss Wells smiled. Then other pupils gave their answers. But John was not listening. Since the tiny child had spoken, his heart had felt very heavy. He was thinking of Pal!

He wanted his little dog! He had not realized before how very much he had missed him.   Was the poor old fellow grieving for him, too?

John was going to cry!   And of all things to do, that would be the worst!   He quickly reached for his ruler and began to balance it on his nose, like a clown in the circus.   He must not cry!

But suddenly the ruler fell with a loud clatter to the floor and everyone in the room turned around and looked at John Mason!

Miss Wells kept him in after school, and told him to write a composition on the industries of the New England States.   This John did, but with a mischievous pen.   He wrote:

*The New England States—and Why*
"In the morning you wake up to the sound of an alarm clock.   Where was it made?   In Connecticut.

You put on your shoes.   Where were they made?   In New Hampshire, or in Massachusetts.

You go to breakfast and if you are lucky, you

have buckwheat cakes with maple syrup. From where? From Vermont!

If you are only a little boy, you play with toys. Where were they made? In Massachusetts.

The cotton in your mother's dress came from —where? Massachusetts, or maybe from Maine. She wears jewelry. Where was that made? In Rhode Island.

If she sews up a tear in your pants, the sewing machine she uses was invented by Elias Howe. Where was he born? In Massachusetts.

If you have to cut the lawn, the lawn mower you use was made—where? In New Hampshire. Then you work in your carpenter shop with tools. Where were they made? In Connecticut factories.

On your supper table you find potatoes and fish, great big blueberries and huckleberries. Where do they come from? Maine. Chickens. From where? Rhode Island. Apples? New Hampshire. Cranberries, clams and lobsters? Why, Cape Cod, of course!

After supper your father smokes his pipe with Connecticut tobacco in it. You talk to your friends on a telephone invented by Alexander Graham Bell, of Massachusetts. Or you send a message to some one far away, with a telegram, invented by Samuel Morse, another New Englander.

You go to bed and read a book written by a famous New England author, such as Henry Wadsworth Longfellow or John Greenleaf Whittier.

Then you say goodnight to your dog, if you have one, and go to sleep under your blankets, made in New Hampshire.

Well, many other things come from New England. I come from New England. It is a wonderful land!

JOHN MASON

## CHAPTER IX

# JOHN'S MOTHER WRITES A LETTER

DEAR SON:

*We have had dinner, your father is happy, and I shall now continue my visit with you. I think I left off in Deerfield. Our next stop was Greenfield, on the Mohawk Trail.*

*The Mohawk Trail is a gloriously scenic highway, dipping into friendly valleys and wandering through cosy little New England towns. One of these, Shelburne Falls village, was plucked out of a story book, and its Bridge of Flowers was built for the Fairy Queen.*

*The Trail climbs up and up, and then it asks you to look at the view. Views! Oh, dear! Why must I always stand and gape*

THE BRIDGE OF FLOWERS, SHELBURNE FALLS, MASS.

*at them! If it had not been for that, what I am about to tell you might never have happened!*

*We had passed such beauties of nature*

*that I had been at pains to keep my seat in the car. As it was, I squealed aloud at moments, causing your father to jump like a jack-rabbit.*

*But how could I help it? There were colored leaves in spots suddenly bursting forth in groves of green—brilliant red-headed children in brunette forests. Hydrangeas, I had always thought, were flowers. But in New England they are poodle dogs with white tails!*

*We stopped the car on the summit of a hill and I jumped out. I had to see the view! Yes, and nothing would do but I had to take Father with me! (Father is not terribly fond of views—especially before dinner!)*

*We stood gazing down at the lovely, peaceful country, and the distant, steepled towns, and my thoughts were with the angels! (Your father's, however, were, I fear, with a beefsteak!)*

*We returned to the car and started on our*

A SCENE ON THE MOHAWK TRAIL

*way, and it was then that I missed my hand-bag! My handbag, John, with your map in it! Oh, you cannot imagine how distressed I was!*

*We searched all over the car, but it was not*

LONGFELLOW'S HOUSE, CAMBRIDGE, MASS.

*there. I blamed the beauties of New England for making me lose my head that way. I blamed myself for a silly goose. I even blamed your father for being hungry! I don't know why!*

*Father could not understand my anxiety for he knows that I never carry anything very valuable in my bag.*

*"What did you have in that purse of yours that was so precious?" he asked.*

*"John's map to the treasure!" I answered.*

*And then I suddenly thought of C. F.! He had been following us closely, I knew, although I had not seen his car since we had passed him on the road. Still, one could never tell about that old rascal! He had a habit of turning up, like an evil sprite.*

*I worried silently for some moments, and then I told your father the whole story! He slowed down the car and wrinkled his nose the way you do, too, when you are thinking.*

*"C. F., did you say?" he asked.*

"Yes, C. F." I answered. "That is what he told John to call him. Do you know what it means?"

I sometimes believe that your father knows everything, which is, I suppose, too much to believe of anyone! He laughed.

"No," he replied. "But I wonder if it could mean 'Completely Foolish'?"

He laughed again, but I did not. I was too upset. And then Father did a strange thing. He suddenly stopped the car, hopped out, came around to my side, leaned down, straightened up—and handed me my bag!

"I have seen things fall onto running boards before and ride there quite safely for miles," he said. "Allow me, Madam, to return the purse with the missing mystery map!"

Well, as Shakespeare said, "All's Well That Ends Well," and your map is safe once more, Johnny. Of course I expect Father to tease me for the rest of the trip. But I'll *make the best of that, so long as he will take me to Cape Cod at the end of the journey! We must prove that we are right about the treasure!*

*Your devoted*
MOTHER.

*P.S.  Father just wondered if C. F. could mean "Cuckoo Factory"!*

CHURCH, GRAFTON, MASS.

## CHAPTER X

## JOHN HAS A SURPRISE

On that first school day, after John had written his composition, the teacher announced that she would walk toward home with him.

"My farm is on the way to your Uncle's, John," she said, "and we can keep each other company."

John's face fell. Walk home with the teacher! How tiresome! Still, he tried to smile pleasantly and the result was rather painful.

"Oh, all right," he managed, in a tone with a black wreath around it.

They walked along together in silence until Miss Wells said, "Did you know, John, that

I went to this same little school when I was just your age?"

John had not known it and did not really care very much. But he tried to smile again, this time giving the effect of suffering from a severe stomach ache!

"Now I am teaching the children of some of my old school mates," she went on.

John said "Um," or something like it. Whatever it was, it had very little meaning.

"And I know them all so well," the teacher continued, "that we have no secrets from one another. You are the only one whom I—I don't know, John. But I should like to."

John kicked a stone and mumbled "Mmm," but Miss Wells was not to be dismayed. "Something is bothering you, John," she said. "Perhaps if you were to tell me——"

Before John could utter another odd sound, she hurried on, "When boys misbehave, I usually find it is because they are not very happy!"

MISS WELLS

John could not help stealing a glance at
Miss Wells.  She was pretty, and young, and
—well, smart, too.  Because, of course, she
was right!  John was unhappy.  He was
missing Pal!

"I—I had a dog," he began.

"Yes?" Miss Wells smiled at him, kindly.

"I—I had a very good dog!" John gulped.
"He—he was my dog!"

Miss Wells seemed to be examining the meadow over on the side of the road beyond the stone fence. This was very nice of Miss Wells, John thought, because it gave him a chance to use his handkerchief.

"Would you like to tell me some more?" she asked, when the handkerchief had been returned to John's pocket.

He told her all about Pal, and about the ruined bed quilt, and about Uncle Ned. And when he had finished, the teacher said, "I understand perfectly. Pal was dear to you. I know how I should feel if the one I love were sent away."

"Is he a bull—or a terrier?" asked John, quickly, and he saw a smile flit across her face.

"He is neither," she answered.

John lost some interest.

"I call him my sweetheart," she said.

John lost all interest. In fact, he sniffed. Yet, after all, a girl might like a sweetheart as well as a fellow did a dog, though it was hard to understand!

Since that day, John and Miss Wells had been friends and had often kept each other company on the walks to and from school. John thought it strange that Aunt Prue and Uncle Ned, whose farm was so near the teacher's, had never met Miss Wells. But John did not know that in Maine, people do not mingle much with their neighbors.

The story goes that when an old lady died, it was remarked that a surprising number of people mourned her death. For, just think! She had lived in New England *only* thirty years!

This morning, as John neared the yellow schoolhouse, he saw the teacher standing on the steps. She had arrived early, and she was waving to him excitedly. As he approached, she came to meet him.

"Oh, John," she cried. "Come quickly and see what I have for you in the schoolroom!"

She almost dragged him to the door and when she opened it, something like a brown and white flash bounced upon John. Then a concert of barks started in different keys and Pal's loving tongue spoke to John in affectionate kisses.

John could not say a word. He just stood there and held the little dog close while Pal wriggled with delight.

"I met him on the road this morning on my way to school," said Miss Wells. "He was sniffing along, looking for you. He must have escaped from the town. I read the name 'Pal' on his collar so I knew at once who he was. I took him to school with me because I thought it best that he did not go to your uncle's farm."

John knew just what Miss Wells meant. If Pal had gone to the farm, Uncle Ned would surely have taken him right back to town.

"Would you like to keep him here all day, John?" asked the teacher, and, at once, Miss

JOHN HELD PAL CLOSE.

Wells became a golden goddess in John's eyes.

"Oh, would you let me do that—every day?" he cried.

"Of course," she smiled. "I'm sure he will be quiet if we tie him outside."

"But what shall I do with him after school when I go home, and where will he sleep?" asked John.

Miss Wells frowned and thought a moment.  Then she said, "Why not ask your uncle and aunt to let him sleep in the barn? He could do no harm there and I'm sure they would not object."

John was not so sure of this!  However, he kept his thoughts to himself and made a plan.  It was a bad boy plan and he knew it.  But he just had to keep Pal, and he felt certain that Uncle Ned would not allow him to do so.  Not even in the barn.

So, he decided to hide Pal in the loft of the barn without saying a word to anyone.  He would make the dog a comfortable bed there, tuck him away safely every night, and take him to school every day.

John was delighted with his plan!

## CHAPTER XI

## JOHN GOES TO PORTLAND

John was happier now that Pal was back. Each morning he would call for his dog at the barn and steal away with him to school.

Miss Wells was very kind and allowed Pal to stay in the school yard. She even brought food for him upon occasions, which was a great help to John. It was difficult to smuggle meat and bones out of the house and up to the loft without Aunt Prue seeing him do it.

But there were times when John felt very guilty. He wondered what Miss Wells would say if she knew that he was deceiving his aunt and uncle! They did not know that Pal was a guest in their barn.

109

Today was Saturday and the smell of cows and pine woods greeted John as he walked toward Pal's hiding place, early in the morning.

Most New England barns are jealously clasped to the white, wooden breasts of their farmhouses. But the Hollis barn was not attached. However, it was plain to see that the house looked sharply out of the corner of its green-shuttered eye to make sure that it did not escape!

John was wondering why it is that Maine people say "ba-an" (for "barn") just like the "baa" of a sheep. They also call lakes "ponds." It seemed to John that these "Yankees" had their very own way of talking.

He remembered that his father had once told him how the Yankees got their name. When the white people settled in New England, the Indians tried to say "English." But all they could say was "Yenghees," which fi-

UNCLE NED'S BARN

nally turned into the nickname, "Yankees."

There were corn husks and straw on the floor of the barn. Ducks were gabbling, cows were crunching in a pine grove corral, and in a nearby pen, some pigs were grunting. No sound from the loft, and John felt proud to think that he had trained Pal to be quiet.

He climbed the ladder to the loft and, with his hair full of hay, crouched under the low beams. There was a square window through which a shaft of light made it possible for John to see Pal. The little bulldog was wagging away in his corner, where John had arranged for him a bed of sacks.

He greeted his master with enthusiasm. But John patted the sleek head very soberly. His mind was troubled. There was no school, and how could he expect poor Pal to stay cooped up here all day? He would have to take him off some place and not bring him back until evening.

But what if Aunt Prue or Uncle Ned had made plans for him, or needed him on the farm? Well, the best thing was to hurry and sneak away before they could remember that this was Saturday and he was free!

But, just as if the thought had taken wings and flown over to the farmhouse, John heard Aunt Prue calling:

"John! Oh, John!"

Now, what should he do? Perhaps she just wanted him to run an errand, or chop some wood, or . . .

"John! Where are you?"

Oh, dear! He supposed that if he and Pal tried to slip out of the barn now, Aunt Prue would surely see them.

He cupped Pal's little froggy face in his hand and tipped it up to his own. "Now, be good—and don't bark!" he cautioned.

Pal's round eyes looked lovingly into his master's and became two soft-boiled hearts. John patted him once more and then started down the rickety ladder.

Now, at any other time, John would have wanted to go to Portland, where Uncle Ned made his weekly Saturday trips. But today! What would Pal do without him? Would he whine and bark and perhaps draw Aunt Prue over to the barn? And what would Aunt Prue do with Pal if she found him? Also, what would Uncle Ned do to John?

However, there was nothing to be done

about it, so John went to Portland with Uncle Ned and some of Aunt Prue's chickens. They also took along several crates of big, brown eggs.

Portland is a red brick city. It gave John a wind-swept feeling—a brisk, fresh feeling. He thought the Western Promenade very handsome and he loved the view of the Bay, with its islands and ships.

He saw the house where the poet, Longfellow, lived. He went down to the waterfront and was shown where fish and lobsters are made into canned foods.

At Deering Oaks, there is a lovely children's playground and a doll's house perched on a tiny island in the middle of a lake. John thought of the many islands scattered all over the many Maine lakes. He wanted very much to travel and to see the rest of this beautiful country.

On the way home, John was silent and Uncle Ned would have been astonished if he

FISHING BOATS AT PORTLAND, MAINE

could have read the boy's thoughts. They were busily skipping from his parents and C. F. to Pal and Aunt Prue.

Was C. F. determined to have the treasure? Was that why he kept following John's mother and father? Oh, if Mother could only persuade Father to hurry on to Cape Cod!

Then, how about poor Pal at home on the farm? Had Aunt Prue discovered the little dog's hiding place while he and Uncle Ned were away?

By the time they reached the farm, John had worked himself into such a state that he leapt out of the car before it had even stopped.

Uncle Ned mumbled something about "boys breaking their necks," but by this time John was at the barn. He was climbing the ladder, his heart beating like a tom-tom. Was Pal still there?

He bumped his head on the ceiling in his eagerness to find out. He stumbled and fell sprawling when he reached the top. And, as he tried to arise, he was toppled over again by the wildly excited Pal! No conquering hero could ever have been greeted more joyously!

"Never mind, old fellow," said John, letting the dog bathe his face with kisses. "To-night, when everyone is in bed, I'll take you for a walk!"

Now, the word "walk" is a magic dog-word. Try it on any dog and see! At once, the light in their eyes brightens, while wag-gish things occur in the region of the tail.

John kept his promise to Pal that night, as you shall see. He took him for a walk in the woods.

It was a kind thing to do and Pal appre-ciated it. But, somehow, a boy never is sat-isfied. John spoiled it all and caused a terrible thing to happen by——

But that comes later!

## CHAPTER XII

## JOHN'S MOTHER WRITES A LETTER

DEAR JOHN:

*Forgive me for my silence. There was so little to write about until now. But now! Oh, how much I have to say to you!*

*I am writing this letter as we speed along in our car as fast as the law permits. I do hope you can read the scrawl. For, John dear, we are on a chase! A really wild and exciting chase! Lots and lots has happened since I wrote to you, and at last your father is taking our treasure seriously!*

*He had to remain a while in the town of North Adams, which connects the Mo- hawk Trail with the Taconic Trail. After that we went on to Williamstown.*

118

*This is the home of one of the prettiest colleges I have ever seen.  Williams College, with its fine, brick buildings, well kept lawns, and old trees has an air of peace about it.  I can understand how William Cullen Bryant could have written "Thanatopsis" while a student there.  He was only seventeen years old when he wrote it and it was considered the first great American poem.*

*Nothing unusual occurred during our stay in Williamstown, except that I thought I saw C. F.'s car near our hotel.  But, by the time I had told Father to look, it was gone!*

*Father has, of course, amused himself by teasing me about C. F.  He made up a game trying to find as many silly names as he could for the initials "C. F."  "Cabbage Face," "Curious Fellow," "Charlie Funny," were some of them.*

*But now Father has stopped joking!  He has stopped joking after what happened this evening!*

A NEW ENGLAND CHURCH

*We drove down through Massachusetts and into Connecticut. All along, we passed prim villages, proud of their age and tidiness, their history and charm. In every one is the white-pillared, dignified little church, with its high pointed spire reaching the clouds.*

*Litchfield was the home of Henry Ward Beecher, a great speaker, and brother of*

*Harriet Beecher Stowe, who wrote "Uncle Tom's Cabin." Litchfield also is where the first law school in the United States was founded.*

*More lake lands, and rolling, bright green hills with stone fences. Biting, brisk air. Then to Waterbury, the brass center of the world and where clocks and watches are made.*

*Here we lunched at a most unusual place called The King's Kitchen. The walls are covered with paintings and the waitresses were in historic costumes to match the pictures.*

*Bridgeport is a busy manufacturing town. The Barnum Hotel is named for P. T. Barnum, the circus man. The walls of the hotel restaurant are decorated with circus pictures.*

*Next came New Haven, the "college city," with its famous Yale University, which reminded me of Oxford in old England. The streets of New Haven are shadowed by elm trees and enriched by the splendid vine-covered buildings of the college.*

*We wandered about the lovely courtyards and we saw the statue of Nathan Hale near his old dormitory. Nathan Hale was a spy in the Revolution. Before he was hanged he said, "I regret that I have but one life to give for my country."*

*We left New Haven, driving through more green country to Hartford, capital of Connecticut. Here we visited some of the many great insurance companies. One possesses the largest colonial building in the world.*

*"Asylum" is a strange name for a street, isn't it? I found out the reason why it was so named. Hartford, it seems, had the first deaf and dumb asylum in the country and it was built upon that street.*

*But Hartford is far from "deaf and dumb"! It buzzes with busy crowds!*

*Our next stop was Providence, Rhode Is-*

HARKNESS MEMORIAL, NEW HAVEN, CONN.

land.  Though this city is the capital of our smallest state, it is the second largest city in New England.

At last we arrived in Plymouth, where we had expected to spend the night.  I say "had expected"!  For now everything has changed, and here is the reason why!

After we had walked about in the town where the Pilgrims built their first settlement, we visited the shore.  It is called a "stern and rockbound coast."  But it appeared very mild.  To me, the only rockbound part of it was the courage of those wonderful people who landed here so long ago.

In that first cold winter nearly half of the Pilgrims died.  Those who remained planted wheat upon the graves so the Indians would not know how few settlers there were left.

We looked at the statue of Massasoit, a tall, finely built Indian, who was called Protector and Preserver of the Pilgrims.

*Then we saw the famous rock where the Pilgrims landed when they came from England on the Mayflower. Later, when this large rock was being raised, it split into two pieces. The people thought this a sign of the coming separation of the Colonies from England.*

*Part of the rock was placed in Pilgrim Hall. The other part may be seen at the harbor, as it lies in state with a handsome dome above it.*

*Father and I stood there a long time, just thinking and saying nothing. At last Father spoke.*

*"I'm afraid that all good things must end," he said. "I have had word from home and we must turn toward Boston tomorrow. But this is a rather fine place to end a fine trip, isn't it?"*

*I caught my breath and stared at him. So we were not going to Cape Cod! Not going to follow the trail of your map, John!*

*"Oh, we must go to Cape Cod!" I cried. "Think of how disappointed Johnny will be if we don't!"*

*"Why?" asked Father, with that mischievous twinkle in his eye. I knew perfectly well that he knew what I meant.*

*"Because of this, of course!" I answered, and pulled your map out of my purse.*

*A wind was blowing, and just as Father started to take the map from me, it flew out of our hands and down the beach!*

*It whirled along and we started after it when, suddenly,—what do you think happened? None other than C. F. sprang out of nowhere! Yes, nowhere! Unless he had been hiding all that time, waiting his chance! He stooped, picked up the map, ran and was gone!*

*A minute later I heard a motor start, sputter, roar, and fade away. Your father and I had stood there like dummies. It had all gone so quickly—just like the puff of wind* that had blown the map out of our hands.

I must admit that I began to cry. I couldn't help it. I thought of you! Your father put his arm about my shoulders and I saw that his face had become grave.

"Now, don't worry, my dear," he said, "and come along quickly. We'll get into our car, and follow that little scamp to Cape Cod! Because that's surely where he's bound for!"

I dried my eyes. "Then we are not going home?" I asked.

"No," said Father. "Not until we track down this mystery. There may be more to John's fairy story treasure than I had thought. Something not so mysterious, perhaps, but which that little Crab Face knows about! Come along, dear—hurry!"

We hurried. And we are hurrying now. And I only hope you can read this scrawl, because my pen is bouncing up and down on the paper.

*We have not yet overtaken C. F. But then, he may be hiding from us and we have passed him, which is more likely. But, anyway, I know from having studied the map with you, just where to go when we reach Cape Cod. We shall not allow that dreadful little man to beat us to the treasure!*

*Oh, dear! I'm being jiggled about like a bowl of jelly! I must stop writing and mail this. More soon, dear.*

*Lovingly,*

YOUR BOUNCING MOTHER.

PLYMOUTH ROCK, PLYMOUTH, MASS.

CHAPTER XIII

## JOHN PLAYS WITH MATCHES

Everyone was in bed. John could hear Uncle Ned snoring loudly, like a swarm of angry, giant bees.

John put on his clothes and went out to meet the night—and Pal. He let himself into the barn through the window of old Nancy's stall. Nancy gave a snort. But when John spoke to her she said, "Oh, it's you! Very well!" (In horse language, of course!) and settled down once more.

When Pal was released from his prison, he sniffed the night air as though he had never known a whiff of it before. He pranced and ran and jumped like a busy

PAL SNIFFED THE NIGHT AIR.

humming bird—if a rather fat bulldog can be compared to a bird!

It was a glorious night. Pine trees, like thin, pointed witches' hats, pricked a sky lightened by starry peep holes.

John walked along with his hands in his pockets, fingering the many odd objects in those pockets. Among them were two matches.

Now, someone has said that "a boy and a

match should never attach." Well, what happened on this night will prove that to be true!

Finally John walked Pal back to the barn. It was not too dark to see, but John thought it was. The reason for this, no doubt, was because he had two matches in his pocket! So, he struck one of these matches and really believed that without it he could not have seen Pal to bed.

A barn, of course, is full of hay and straw. John's first match went out (or so he thought), and he threw it down and lighted the other.

He held the flame up high and watched Pal snuggle down on his sacks in the corner. Then he climbed down the ladder, blew out his second match, and left the barn.

When John was in bed with the covers pulled up to his chin, he shut his eyes and started to drop into sleepland. But suddenly he was awake again and there was a strange flickering light in his room. It danced all over like red shadows. Then John heard voices outside, mingled with a crackling sound.

He jumped out of bed and ran to the window. The barn was in flames! He recognized Uncle Ned, leading a horse out of the burning building.

Pal! Pal in the barn! Oh, how horrible! And nobody knew! Nobody had any idea that a little dog was there! If Pal would only bark! But John remembered how well he had trained him not to!

Cold with fear, the boy ran down the stairs and out of the house, dressed only in his pajamas and with bare feet.

Now he is running toward the barn. And now he is inside the burning building. He cannot see the loft ladder. How dreadful the smoke is! He gropes his way and thinks he is close. He begins to cough. Oh, that smoke!

And then he feels a man's strong arms pick him up. Screaming and kicking, he is carried outside in the air, just as the ladder to the loft falls down in a flaming heap.

"Oh, John, why did you do that?" Aunt Prue stands over him like the tall broomstick with which she punishes the dirt each morning.

The barn was burning brightly now. The fire department had arrived and was fighting the flames. But everyone knew that it would be hopeless.

Uncle Ned was mopping his brow with a big, red handkerchief. John's head throbbed. He felt dizzy. He could not speak. It was Uncle Ned who had pulled him out of danger, he knew. But Uncle Ned was looking at him now as if he were some kind of creature in a zoo.

"It is often difficult to fathom the ways of a boy," he remarked to his wife. Then he added, "Well, the live things are all safe at

LONG LAKE, NEAR NAPLES, MAINE

any rate, and we won't let the house burn.
So we're ever so fortunate."

John clutched his uncle's coat.  The live
things were safe, he had said!

"Oh, Uncle Ned, did you see my dog?" he cried.

Uncle Ned looked at John, this time, the way people peer at freaks in a side show. "Of course I did not!" he answered. "You know as well as I do that I took the dog to town last week!"

"But—he's in the barn, Uncle Ned! Pal's in the barn! Oh, please let me go!" John tried to break away, but his aunt and uncle held him.

Then, suddenly, there was a crash. The barn roof had collapsed!

With a jerk, and a sob, John pulled away from his aunt and uncle, and ran toward the barn. But he could not get near it. Hot waves struck him in the face and a fireman pushed him back, swearing loudly.

John turned and stumbled in the direction of the house.

It was all his fault! He should have told Uncle Ned before he hid Pal in the loft.

Even if Uncle Ned had taken Pal to town again, and John had been unhappy, the poor little dog would now be alive! He would not have been trapped in a burning barn because his master had been disobedient and deceitful! Oh, poor little Pal!

John found his way to his room, threw himself across the bed, and for several moments, all he could hear were his own sobs.

Then, gradually, it came to him that someone was talking under his window. He listened, his face still hidden in the pillow.

"I can't think how it could have happened—" Uncle Ned's voice. "Of course, sometimes a tramp does get into a barn and drops a lighted match——"

A lighted match! John had done it! John had set the barn on fire himself!

He raised himself on his elbow to listen some more, but the voices had died away.

John brushed his sleeve across his eyes and got down off the bed. He would go right to Uncle Ned and tell him everything! He would tell him about Pal and the matches and——

He opened the door and started out of his room, but stopped. Or rather, he was stopped by what appeared to be an electric body, hurling itself upon him.

It was a short, plump, brown and white body. It leaped up and it fell back; it leaped up again, until John caught it in his arms. Then it covered his face with wet, whiskery kisses.

John did not know or care how it had all happened. Pal was alive and in his arms again!

But Pal did know. He knew all about it. He had not liked being in that barn because something very unpleasant had happened there. First of all, smoke had tickled his sensitive nose and made him sneeze. Then, dreadful heat had made him pant uncomfortably.

Now, Pal was not a jumping dog. But there was a square window in front of the loft, high off the ground, and he had realized that the only thing to do was to use it!

Horrible, crackling sounds had reached his ears. Then red tongues had begun to lick their way toward him, and he had panted harder and harder.

So he had gathered himself into a round, courageous ball and jumped. He had landed safely and the next question had been, "Where is the One I Love?"

This had not been difficult to answer because of an excellent nose. Pal had sniffed about until he had found his way to the room belonging to the One He Loved. Then he had sat outside the door.

He had whined softly, but he could hear the One He Loved whining, too. So he had waited until the door opened and then he had greeted his master, hoping all the time that he had not done the wrong thing!

Evidently, he had not, because his master did not scold.  Instead, he patted him gently and said, "Good old fellow!" over and over, which always meant pleasant things.

Then, suddenly, his master exclaimed, "I'm going to tell Uncle Ned everything right now!"  And together they dashed out of the room and down the stairs!

STREET IN NAPLES, MAINE

## CHAPTER XIV

## JOHN'S MOTHER WRITES A LETTER

DEAR SON:

*We are home again! We drove into Boston over the Charles River from Cambridge, where Father had to stop—on business, of course.*

*It was good to see the gold dome of our proud State House, shining a welcome above the beehive of brick rooftops.*

*While in Cambridge, I spent the time visiting Harvard University. The first college built in America, today it is one of the largest universities in the country. Many famous men, among them three Presidents of the United States, have graduated from there.*

*I enjoyed walking the streets of Cam-*

HARVARD UNIVERSITY, CAMBRIDGE, MASS.

bridge. The fine old houses have elm tree shadows all over their faces. Their over-hanging roofs look like the brows of wise men.

But here I am, like all mystery writers, "keeping you in suspense," as they say! For, what you really want to know is how our adventure ended.

When I left off, your father and I were

*racing along toward Cape Cod, weren't we? We felt sure that we had passed C. F.'s cracker-box car on the road, as Father had driven very fast. So we expected to have plenty of time to explore Provincetown before the old man's arrival.*

*At first the road led through sea-salty country of many trees and peaked roof houses.*

*It is curious to see the map creatures of our imaginations come to life. On the map, the Cape is a long, narrow strip of land. I once heard the following legend about it.*

*The Indians believed that a giant used Cape Cod for his bed, and the mark of his body gave the land its shape.*

*Once the giant fell asleep and when he awoke he found his shoes full of sand. He threw the sand out into the ocean and it formed two islands, Nantucket and Martha's Vineyard.*

*Although this is a legend, the two islands*

*make very beautiful summer playgrounds.*

*Cape Cod was named because of the many codfish, which sometimes are called the "Cape Cod turkey."*

*All at once Father slapped the wheel of the car and cried, "I have it!"*

*"What have you?" I gasped. (I thought surely he must have solved the mystery!)*

*"C. F. stands for Cod Fish!" he said, grinning from ear to ear.*

*I was furious. Joking at a time like this!*

*"Oh, but you are beginning to believe in John's treasure, aren't you?" I asked him, seriously.*

*"I am beginning to believe," he replied, "that something much more real is drawing Cat Fish—I mean, Cod Fish,—to Provincetown with that map! As for the childish notion of a hidden treasure—well, I am beginning to believe that you should be called 'M. G.'"*

*"What does that mean?" I asked.*

*"Mother Goose!"* he replied.

*Oh, well, Mother Goose was a very fine lady who lived in Boston years ago. She wrote those beloved little nursery rhymes for her own grandchild. Perhaps some day I shall make up mystery stories for my grandchildren. Who knows?*

*It was growing darker and darker, but we could see as we drew closer to the tip of the Cape, that the country became more sandy. We had also been passing many houses where brightly painted toys were on sale.*

*When we reached Provincetown it was quite dark. I could only imagine the long, thin tongue of land which reached out into the water to greet the Pilgrims when they had first arrived from England.*

*Do you recall the words that were written on our map? "House on corner, below hill?" Well, that was the house I planned to find!*

*The Pilgrim Memorial Monument is at the*

THE PILGRIM MEMORIAL MONUMENT,
PROVINCETOWN, MASS.

*top of a winding hill, which I believe must be
the hill mentioned on the map.  So we steered
for that spot.  But when we reached it we
found there a modern public school!*

*However, just across the street was a very
old, red house, badly in need of paint.  I got*

*out of the car, crossed the street, and Father followed me.*

*Not a light in the house, and surely not a soul in it either! Who would want to live in such a place? The windows were without glass. An old-fashioned cupola on top looked like a lopsided crown on the head of some dethroned monarch. It was a sorry sight.*

*But just the same, I rang the bell. As I expected, nobody came to the door.*

*We went into the town and made inquiries about the house. It seemed that it belonged to a sea captain who lived in Barnstable, which is the main Cape Cod town. There are fifteen of these towns, all divided into villages, the most important of which is Hyannis.*

*They told us that the house was one of the oldest in Provincetown. It had been deserted for a long time. But in the past days, it had belonged to an important family named—Mason! What do you think of that, John Mason?*

*Of course I grew frightfully excited. I felt sure that this "important old family" had been ancestors of Father's!*

*But do you think Father showed the least interest? No indeed! He only looked bored and said, 'No ancestor of mine was ever important!'*

*We went back to the house to wait for C. F. and the map. After that? Well, my private plan was to break in! It would be easy enough because of the many openings in the house. And it would not be wrong because the place was empty. Anyway, we were only after what rightfully belonged to us—or rather, to you!*

*However, Father looked so fierce that I hesitated suggesting anything. I knew that he had one idea in mind—to catch C. F. and to make the little man explain his strange actions!*

*It was dreary, waiting there in the darkness. I did so want to wander about the narrow streets and see the fishing wharves of*

Provincetown. I had heard that artists flock to this charming little spot, and I was eager to know it better.

Still, I could hardly wait to enter the house and start my search for the treasure! I thought I should know just where to look, for I had studied the map so often with you.

But there stood Father, looking like a policeman!

Presently, I could stand it no longer and I sneaked off in the direction of one of the broken windows.

"Where are you going?" asked Father.

"Into the house!" I said. And, before he could call me back, in I went!

Now, don't you think that was brave of me, John?

I groped my way to the basement and told myself that there was nothing to fear. But I admit, I did not believe myself at all! My knees were trembling as I went down the rickety old stairs, and all at once I beheld

"A PURITAN IN THE STOCKS"—AN UNUSUAL
DISPLAY ON CAPE COD

*two gleaming things shining up at me.*
*I almost let out a scream and turned back.*
*But the gleams did not move, so I took cour-*
*age, went closer, and discovered that they*
*belonged to a stuffed owl!  They were the*
*glass eyes of an old stuffed bird which used*

*to be a fashionable ornament years ago!*

*You remember that the map gave no plan of the basement. It only showed the house with a cross marked where we believed the basement to be. So I wandered about, feeling my way like a blind person, not knowing where to look first.*

*And, as I was wandering, I thought I heard footsteps in the house above me! My heart leaped. But before it had time to hop right out of my mouth, your father's voice called to me. Oh, how relieved I was!*

*Father came down the stairs and into the basement. In one hand he held a powerful flashlight, and with the other he clasped the thin little claw of—C. F.!*

*Father was smiling. Yes, actually smiling good-naturedly.*

*"My dear," he exclaimed. "I want you to meet my friend, C. F.!"*

*I shook hands with the little man, who bowed politely.*

*Father went on. "Here is the map," he said, and pulled it out of his pocket. "C. F. really meant no harm at all, which you will agree when you have heard what those initials stand for. Then you will understand everything as I do!"*

*"But how—why—" I wanted to know so many things that I couldn't even ask one question without stammering.*

*Father laughed. "Never mind questions now," he said. "The main thing is to search for the treasure. And C. F. will help us!"*

*I could hardly believe that it was your father talking!*

*We all searched as hard as we could, each going his own way in different parts of the basement.*

*We worked thus for some time. Just when I was beginning to wonder if there really was a treasure, C. F. gave a cry from a corner where he had been pottering around. We rushed over to him. He held something in his hand which he told us he had found behind a loose board in the wall.  It was the treasure!*

*But, once again I am going to be horrid and "keep you in suspense."  Not for very long, however, because almost as soon as this letter reaches you, C. F. will be back in Naples.*

*C. F. is bringing the treasure to you and will explain everything.  And then, dear, you must come home, for your father and I have missed you a great deal.  So let us know what train to meet!*

*With love to you, Aunt Prue and Uncle Ned,*

YOUR DEVOTED MOTHER.

*And your Detective Father (Hush!)*

## CHAPTER XV

# JOHN WRITES A LETTER

*Naples, Maine.*

DEAR MOTHER AND FATHER:

*C. F. came back.   He brought the treasure
and I never did see such a fine toy clipper
ship!   It's a perfect model of the old sailing
vessels our ancestors used.   I like it better
than anything I own—except Pal, of course!*

*Pal is back again.   Uncle Ned lets me
keep him here.   And he's behaving himself,
too.   Not Uncle Ned!   I mean Pal!*

*But Uncle Ned likes me better than he did
at first, I think, and I like him, too.   He says
I am honest, because I told him everything.
He wants me to ask you if I can stay here
until after Thanksgiving.*

JOHN WRITES A LETTER.

*He says that every year they have a feast at the farm. It is to celebrate the first Thanksgiving, when the Colonists invited the Indians, after the first harvest. So he's invited me!*

*Aunt Prue makes pickles and all kinds of pies, and of course there'll be a turkey and everything. So please let me stay!*

*C. F. told me what his initials stand for.*

*He believes in all mysteries and fairy tales and he never could bear to see a child laughed at. That must be why he took so much trouble for me!*

*You know, he says that on the day when he found me crying, after you left, he made up his mind to help me. So he followed you to scare you, and to make Father serious about the treasure and send him on to Cape Cod!*

*We have a big pot of pork and beans for breakfast every Sunday morning, and steamed brown bread, and it lasts for days (if Aunt Prue locks it up)!*

*I wonder if Mary, William and Ned Mason really did hide the clipper ship treasure? Since I found out what C. F. stands for, I think maybe he had something to do with it. What do you think?*

*One of the meals I like best is a boiled dinner. Aunt Prue boils corned beef and cabbage and all kinds of vegetables together and it's good!  Please let me stay a little longer!*

*I am going to invite C. F. for Thanksgiving dinner.  Uncle Ned says he wants to meet the "Children's Friend"!*

*Your loving*

JOHN.

*P.S.  I am being very good.*

*P.S.  I burned the barn down.*

### THE END